SESAME STREET

Elmo's ULTIMATE EDITION STORYBOOK

Dalmatian Kids, LLC, 2007. All rights reserved.
Published by Dalmatian Kids, LLC, 2007. The DALMATIAN KIDS name and logo
are trademarks of Dalmatian Publishing Group, LLC, Franklin, Tennessee 37067.
No part of this book may be reproduced or copied in any form
without written permission from the copyright owner.

Dalmatian
KIDS

Printed in Guangzhou, Guangdong, China
ISBN: 1-61524-388-7

10 11 12 13 GF35920 10 9 8 7 6 5 4 3 2

Elmo Loves You!

By Sarah Albee • Illustrated by Maggie Swanson

Everyone loves something.
Babies love noise.
Birds love singing.

Kids love toys.

Bert loves pigeons,
and pigeons love to coo.
Can you guess who Elmo loves?
Elmo loves *you!*

Piggies love to roll in mud.

Penguins love the snow.

Farmers love to wake up early.
Roosters love to crow.

Zoe loves the library. Grover loves it, too.
Elmo whispers quietly, "Elmo loves *you!*"

The Count loves counting things.

Ernie loves to drum.

Monsters love to exercise.

Kids love bubble gum.

Natasha and her daddy love playing peekaboo.
But—*psssst!*—before you turn the page...
Elmo loves *you!*

Everyone loves something.
Elmo told you this was true.
And now you know who Elmo loves:
Elmo loves *you!*

Before Elmo ends his poem,
Elmo wants to ask you this:
Will you be Elmo's valentine?
Can Elmo have a kiss?

THE END

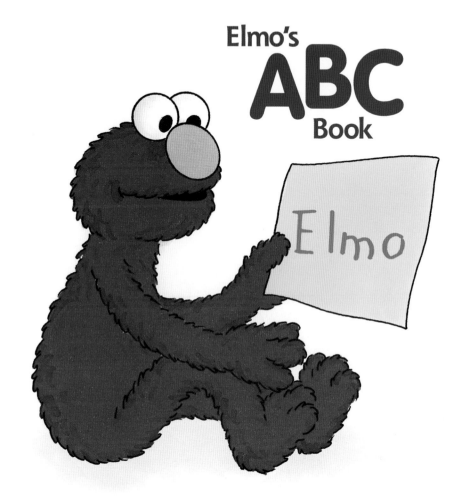

Elmo's ABC Book

By Sarah Albee • Illustrated by Tom Brannon

Hello! Elmo is trying to decide
what Elmo's favorite letter is.
Will you help Elmo?

Oh, thank you!

Elmo loves apples
because they are delicious and crunchy.
And apples start with the letter **A**.
So **A** must be Elmo's favorite letter.

But wait! Baby starts with the letter **B**.
And Elmo loves babies, too. So **B** must be
Elmo's favorite letter. Right, baby?

Crayon and cat begin with the letter **C**.
So Elmo thinks that maybe **C** is Elmo's
favorite letter.

Oh, but Elmo LOVES dogs! Hello, doggies!
And doggie starts with the letter **D**.

Uh, oh! Elmo just remembered that
Elmo's name begins with the letter **E**.

But Elmo's fur is very fuzzy and fluffy.
So **F** must be Elmo's favorite letter!

But green grapes make a great snack.

And grapes begin with the letter **G**!

Coming home for a hug
is one of Elmo's favorite things.
So **H** must be the one.
Ha ha ha! Tee hee hee!

Oh, but Elmo loves
to use Elmo's imagination!
And **I** is the first letter
in imagination!

Could it be **J**? Elmo is a very good joke teller.
Would you like to hear Elmo's joke?

Knock, knock.
Who's there?
Boo.
Boo who?
Please don't cry.

Elmo just realized
that kangaroo starts
with the letter **K**.

How do you do,
little kangaroo?

Oh, but L is the first letter in the word love.

Elmo just *loves* love!

Monster starts with **M**.

Elmo is a little monster and so are Elmo's friends.

So **M** must be Elmo's favorite letter.

Elmo can make a lot of noisy noise! Wheeee!!!

And so can an octopus.

Do you think N or O could be Elmo's favorite letter?

P is the first letter in the word poem.

And Elmo just wrote this poem called

"Q is for Quilt."

Is **Q** Elmo's favorite letter?

Elmo also loves riddles:

What did the sea say to the sand?
Nothing. It just waved.

R must be Elmo's favorite letter!

Can Elmo tell you a secret?

Elmo thinks that you have a very nice smile.

So maybe **S** is Elmo's favorite letter.

Turtles are terrific! And guess what?
Turtle begins with a T.

Toodle-oo, turtle!

Toodle-oo!

Ha ha ha! Hee hee hee!
Elmo is upside-down.

And Elmo likes to
listen to the violin!
So is Elmo's favorite letter
U? Or is it **V**?

Elmo wishes he could decide which is his favorite
letter. What about **W**? Or **X**?
Could it be **Y**?
Why, oh why, can't Elmo decide!

THE END

ELMO'S First Babysitter

By Sarah Albee • Illustrated by Tom Brannon

Elmo is so excited! Elmo is going to have a babysitter tonight! Her name is Emily. There's the doorbell! That must be Emily!

Um, wait a minute. Maybe Elmo doesn't really want a babysitter after all.

It *is* Emily. She looks nice, doesn't she? Elmo's mommy and daddy wrote down the phone number of the place they're going tonight. And they also wrote the phone numbers of our neighbors, just in case. Now it's time to hug Mommy and Daddy good-bye.

Restaurant
555-9423

Neighbors
555-9641
555-8003

Did you see what we made? Kooky faces! Elmo made this
one all by himself!

Wow! Elmo likes this music!

Elmo's toe feels all better now. And look—
Emily brought bubbles for Elmo to play with in
the bathtub. When Mommy and Daddy give
Elmo a bath, we don't ever get to blow bubbles.

Good morning, Mommy! Good morning, Daddy!
Elmo liked having a babysitter! It was fun!
When is Emily coming back?

THE END

It's Check-up Time, Elmo!

Original story by Sarah Albee • Illustrated by Tom Brannon
Contributing writers: Elizabeth Clasing and P.J. Shaw

"Why is Elmo going to visit the doctor today?" Elmo asked one morning, as his mommy buckled the little monster into his car seat. "Elmo doesn't feel sick!"

"It's check-up time," Elmo's mommy reminded him. "You need a check-up even when you feel well. The doctor makes sure you're growing and staying healthy. She'll check your ears and eyes, and listen to your heart, too."

Elmo touched the fuzzy red fur over his heart. "Oooh! Elmo wonders what *that* sounds like."

"Today you'll find out," Mommy promised.

In the waiting room, Elmo saw a little green monster he knew.
"Lily! Are you here for a check-up, too?"
"No, I have a tummy ache," she said in a small voice, watching him play with some paper and crayons.
Elmo drew Lily a silly picture to make her smile.
"Will the doctor help Lily feel better?" Elmo asked his mommy.
"I'm sure she will," Mommy answered.

Just then, nurse Rhonda came in. Elmo liked her braided hair.
Rhonda smiled a great big smile when she saw Elmo.
    "Your turn next, Elmo!" she said.
    Later, Elmo followed Rhonda into the examining room.
    Rhonda smiled. "Hop up onto the scales, Elmo," she told him.
"Let's see how much you've grown."

Rhonda was surprised at how much taller Elmo was since last time. "Elmo is a big monster now," he said happily.

Rhonda checked Elmo's eyes next.

Then she wrapped a cushion around Elmo's arm to test his blood pressure. He watched it puff up and down. "Just like a balloon!" Elmo giggled.

After that, Dr. Diane came in. She asked Elmo about his pet fish, Dorothy, while she washed her hands.

"Maybe Dorothy needs a check-up, too," Elmo said. "Is there a doctor for fish?"

"Animal doctors are called veterinarians," said Dr. Diane. "But fish don't need check-ups like we do."

Elmo thought about that. "It would be hard to test Dorothy's ears and eyes. They're so tiny!"

"And I would need a scuba suit to give her a check-up," Dr. Diane said with a grin.

That made Elmo laugh!

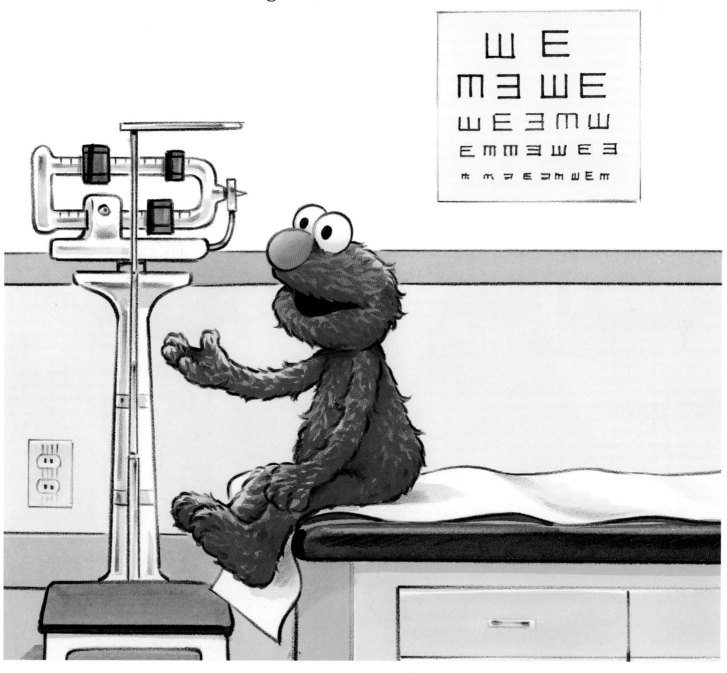

Dr. Diane had a few more tests to give Elmo. She checked his reflexes first. The doctor tap-tap-tapped softly under Elmo's knee until his furry red leg suddenly jumped!

"Ha-ha! That feels so funny," Elmo giggled.

Then she took his temperature with a thermometer.

"Not too hot and not too cold," the doctor said with a smile. "Elmo is just right!"

The doctor checked Elmo's ears with a little light, then his throat. "Open wide, Elmo," she said. Elmo went "*aaah*."

Next, Dr. Diane asked him to lie down so she could feel his tummy for any aches.

It tickled a little! Elmo tried hard not to giggle until Dr. Diane was through.

Dr. Diane checked Elmo's back, and then said,
"Time to listen to your breathing and your heart, Elmo."

"Yay! Elmo was wondering what a heart sounds like," Elmo exclaimed.

Dr. Diane listened with her stethoscope as Elmo took deep breaths. Then she moved it around to hear Elmo's heart. "This is what I hear," she said. "Thump-*thump*. Thump-*thump*. Thump-*thump*."

"Elmo's heart sounds like a drum!" said Elmo.

"That's right. Your heart sounds very strong," said Dr. Diane. "Run and play every day and it will get even stronger."

Elmo nodded happily. He could do that!

Finally, Dr. Diane asked Elmo some questions:
"Do you wear a bike helmet to stay healthy and safe? Do you ride in a car seat? Do you make sure a grown-up is watching when you go swimming or cross the street?"
Elmo answered yes to every one.

"And do you get plenty of rest?" the doctor asked Elmo.

He nodded. "Elmo does! And Elmo will make sure Mommy does, too."

Elmo's mommy laughed at that. "Thank you, Elmo," she said.

"Sometimes we need a shot during a check-up. The medicine keeps us safe from things that make us sick," Dr. Diane said. She looked into a folder with Elmo's name on it. "I see that you need one of those today, Elmo."

Elmo remembered getting a shot one time. He pointed to his arm. "It went right here," Elmo told nurse Rhonda. "It felt like a little pinch, that's all."

Elmo's mommy smiled proudly at Elmo while he got his shot.

"Dr. Diane is good at giving shots," she said, "but you were a very brave monster anyway, Elmo."

That made Elmo feel good. Then Elmo remembered something else. "Hey, Elmo got a sticker last time!"

Dr. Diane laughed. "You may have a special one today, too."

"Well, Elmo, that's it," said Dr. Diane. "We're done with your check-up."

Elmo waved good-bye happily. He liked knowing he was strong and healthy.

"Thanks, Dr. Diane," he said. "Elmo was feeling okay before his check-up, but now Elmo feels even better!"

Nurse Rhonda's Check-up Tips

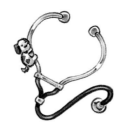

POSITIVE THOUGHTS Let your child know that doctors and nurses are there to help us feel better and to keep us healthy and strong!

INFORMATION Explain to your child that sometimes she will go to the doctor even when she feels okay, because regular check-ups help her stay healthy. You might say, "The nurse will call you from the waiting room and check your height, weight, blood pressure, and temperature. Later, the doctor will listen to your heart and lungs with a long, funny-looking instrument called a stethoscope, and examine your ears, nose, throat, and eyes with a light. The doctor might also check the reflexes in your knees with a little rubber hammer."

HONESTY It's important to be honest with your child about what he should expect during a doctor visit, even if it means talking about a shot. Say, "It may sting, but just for a little bit."

COMFORT Comforting words and actions are important, particularly if your child is injured or ill. Talk in a soothing voice and ask what would "make it better." Suggest that your child bring a doll or stuffed animal along on a visit to the doctor or hospital to make her feel more comfortable.

MAKE BELIEVE Pretending to be a doctor or nurse can help prepare a child for doctor visits. "Examine" the eyes, ears, and mouth of a favorite stuffed animal or doll, like Elmo. Encourage your child to take care of the toy by giving it lots of comfort and attention. Help tuck the doll into bed, for instance, and tell it to get lots of rest. Show your child how to blow the doll's nose, rub its tummy, and share a book. And ask some caring questions: "Did you eat a good breakfast today and drink lots of water? Did you take a nap? Will you come back for a check-up real soon?"

PRACTICE Help your child listen to your heart by hugging her close and placing her ear against your chest. Explain that a doctor or nurse will probably listen to her heart during a visit, but with a stethoscope.

"Elmo loves getting a check-up, and Elmo loves YOU!"

THE END

ELMO VISITS THE DENTIST

By P.J. Shaw • Illustrated by Tom Brannon

"Ow-ow-owoo**OOO**!" howled the Big Bad Wolf one day. "I just want to huff and puff and—and—*blow something in!*" He plopped down on a bench, rubbing his chinny-chin-chin. "What's wrong, Big Bad?" asked one of the three little pigs. "I have a too**OOOO**thache!" the wolf complained.

"The dentist helps to take care of Elmo's teeth," said Elmo. "Elmo is pretty sure the dentist can help wolf teeth, too."

"That's right," said Abby Cadabby. "My aunt says going to the dentist makes you feel better. And *she's* the tooth fairy, so she should know!"

"Wait! Elmo has an idea," said Elmo. "Abby can do magic! She could make a toothache go away with her training wand."

"I can't *poof* away a toothache, Elmo," said Abby. "I can only turn things into pumpkins. See?" And she waved her wand at a soccer ball: "*Lumpkin, bumpkin, diddle-diddle dumpkin, zumpkin, frumpkin, PUMPKIN!!!*"

Big Bad jumped nervously as the soccer ball turned into a pumpkin. "Elmo was right," said Big Bad. "I need a dentist—not magic." "When Big Bad goes to the dentist, Elmo will go with him," Elmo said.

So, the next day, the Big Bad Wolf, Elmo, and Elmo's mommy all went to see Dr. Bradley. In the waiting room, Elmo saw lots of picture books and toys—even an aquarium!

"Ah-oowooOOOO!" Big Bad yowled every now and then.

His toothache was only a teeny bit worse, but he was a wolf and couldn't help himself.

"The dentist will make your tooth better," Elmo's mommy said gently.

"Big Bad Wolf!" called the dental assistant, Miss Stella.
Big Bad whimpered, and Elmo felt worried about his friend.
"We'll take good care of him," Miss Stella told Elmo. "But why don't you come along and keep him company?"

"Good idea!" Elmo agreed. "Elmo can't wait to see how the dentist takes care of *wolf* teeth!"

Miss Stella smiled. "We take care of Big Bad Wolf teeth the same way we take care of little red monster teeth."

"Elmo, let's pretend *you're* having a check-up, so Big Bad can see what happens," said Miss Stella. "Climb up in the dentist's chair and I'll give you a ride."

"Woooo, Elmo is floating," said Elmo, as the chair s-l-o-w-l-y rose.

"Now it's your turn, Big Bad," said Miss Stella.

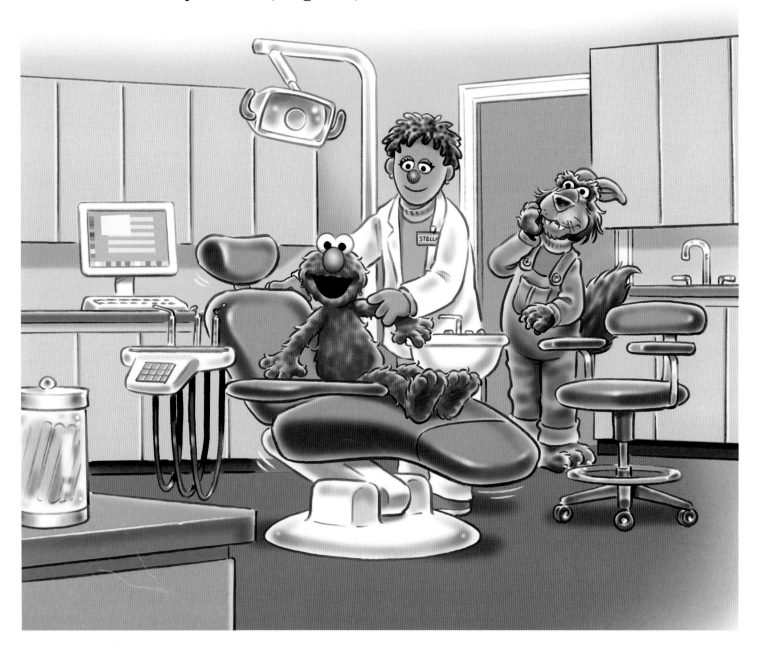

"Will Big Bad get a bib?" Elmo said, remembering his last visit.

"A bib? A baby bib?!" barked the wolf. "Whattaya mean? I'm too BIG! It says so right in my name."

Elmo giggled. "No, silly! It's to keep Big Bad from getting messy when Miss Stella cleans his teeth."

"And *I* wear a mask and gloves to protect little monsters—and big bad wolves—from germs," added Miss Stella.

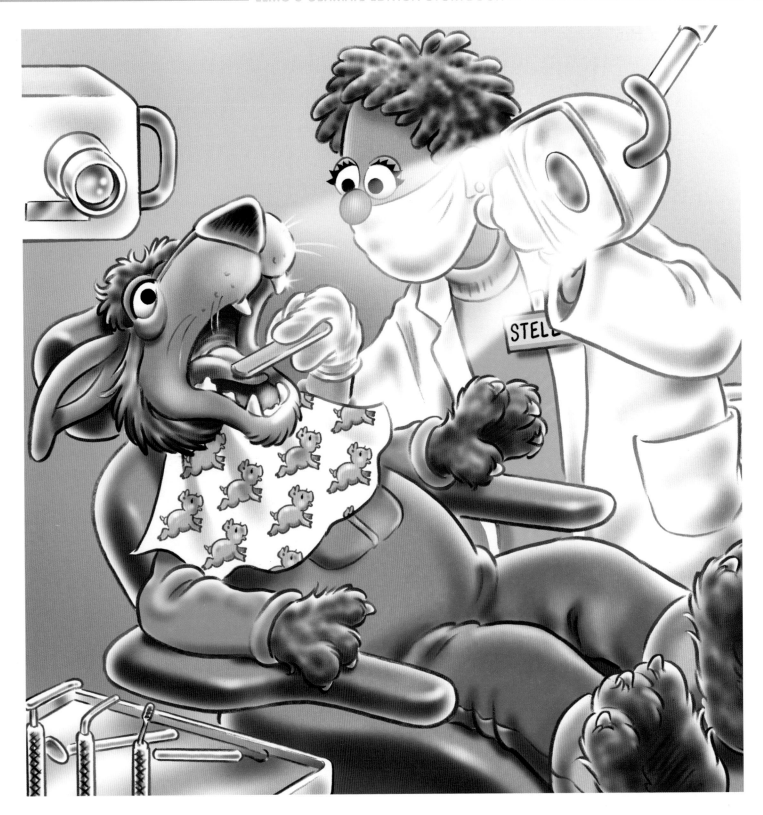

Big Bad lay back in the chair, and Miss Stella pulled down a light.
"It's pretty dark in there," Elmo said.

"Holy molars!" Miss Stella joked. "What big teeth you have!

"Now," she added seriously, "we take X-rays—little pictures of your teeth. Then we brush your teeth to chase away any sugar bugs."

"*Bugs*?" Elmo exclaimed. "Like in Oscar's trash can?!? *Ewwwww!*"

"I mean things like sugar that might start a cavity—a little hole in your tooth. They're not *really* bugs," Miss Stella laughed.

"Ah ew at," mumbled Big Bad. (That's what "I knew that" sounds like with your mouth open wide.)

"Let's pick a yummy toothpaste," said Miss Stella. "What flavor do you like, Big Bad—cinnamon, peppermint, or bubblegum?"

"Ubbleum!" gurgled the wolf with his mouth still open.

"I'll put the toothpaste on this little brush and then we'll tickle your teeth," Miss Stella explained.

"A toothbrush that tickles your teeth. A toothbrush that tickles your teeth!" Elmo chanted. "Just *saying* that makes Elmo feel tickly all over!"

"Feel the brush on your paw—it's very soft," said Miss Stella. "We'll clean between the teeth with skinny string called floss. Then we'll rinse your mouth with a little squirty tool. And, before we're done, we'll look at your tongue and your gums."

"Wow," said Elmo. "That's a mouthful!"

Then Dr. Bradley, the dentist, came in. He gave Big Bad a pat on his shaggy head. "We'll get that tooth fixed right up," he said cheerfully. "Say, Elmo, tell me something: Does a train have teeth?"

"No." Elmo shook his head.

"Then how come it can *CHOO*?!?" Dr. Bradley hooted.

"Woof-woof-woof-woof!" chuckled Big Bad.

"I remember your first check-up, Elmo," said Dr. Bradley. "You were very little. You know, sometimes we even see tiny babies." Then he whispered: "But this is the first time we've ever had a *wolf* in the office."

"Ih mah fuh ahm, hoo," burbled Big Bad, meaning "It's my first time, too."

"My, what big ears you have," Dr. Bradley laughed.

Dr. Bradley asked Elmo to wait outside while he filled Big Bad's cavity. "Don't worry," he told Elmo. "I'll let your friend listen to some fun music while I fix his hurt tooth. How about…Wailin' Jennings!"

When he was finished, Dr. Bradley called Elmo back in, and Big Bad proudly showed off his new filling.

"Now, Big Bad, I don't know what you've been eating," Dr. Bradley said kindly, "but it's given you a cavity."

Big Bad looked sheepish.

"So, from now on, be sure to eat lots of yummy, healthy foods, like cereal, vegetables, and fruit."

"Big Bad and Elmo like bananas!" said Elmo.

"Well, Big Bad, you're all done," said Dr. Bradley. "That filling will stop your toothache."

"Elmo wants to know what happens next, Dr. Bradley," said Elmo.

"Next, we find a time for Big Bad to come back for a check-up. That way, we can stop other cavities before they begin, and he can live happily ever after."

"Thank you, Dr. Bradley," said Elmo.
"Thank yoooOOO!" loudly howled the wolf.
Elmo sighed. "Elmo wishes Big Bad wouldn't do that."

"Here are some new toothbrushes to take with you," said Miss Stella.
"And you get to pick something out of the treasure chest."
Elmo picked a wiggly, squiggly, play worm for his goldfish, Dorothy.
Big Bad Wolf took a toy tea set for Little Red Riding Hood.
"I'm not bad all the time," he told Elmo's mommy.

"Remember to brush for as long as it takes to sing your ABCs twice, in the morning *and* before you go to bed at night," Miss Stella said.

"Elmo and Big Bad promise," said Elmo. "Good-bye!"

The next day, Big Bad Wolf showed off his fangs to everyone.
"My, what big, healthy teeth you have," said Zoe.
"The better to EAT APPLES with!" Big Bad replied, as the three little pigs scampered by.
"Look out!" they squealed gleefully. "He's after our apples!"
And away they raced—crying "wee, wee, wee," all the way home.

THE END

What Makes You Giggle?

By P.J. Shaw • Illustrated by Tom Brannon

W hat makes you giggle,
What gives you a grin?
Big Bird in a tutu doing a spin!

What makes you chuckle,
Or tickles your tummy?
A grouch birthday party—
Where presents are crummy!

Do giraffes give you laughs
On a trip to the zoo?
Or how about chimps?
Monkey-see, monkey-do!

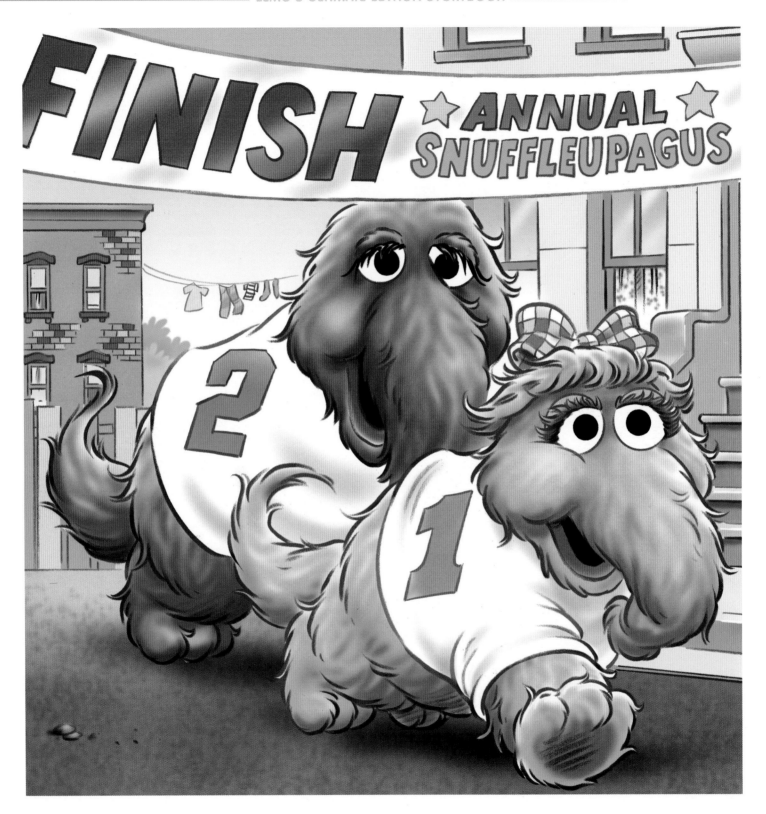

A Snuffleupagus race
Might just give you a smile.
They *galumph* to the finish.
Alice wins by a mile!

What makes you laugh,
What makes you giggle?
A monstrous contest
For noses that wiggle!

Halloween's fun...
And so spooky, you shriek!

Hide-and-seek, trick-or-treat,
Oscar's can—EEK!

What makes you whoop,
Makes you squeal with delight?
A day at the pool,
When the water's just right.

Dive rings and water wings,
Snorkels and masks.
Flippers and floaties,
And fountains that splash!

What makes you snicker,
Guffaw or tee-hee?
A neighborhood cookout
At Nonny Bird's tree?

Make-your-own cupcakes
With milk-chocolate chips?
Maybe strawberries, raisins,
Or cinnamon bits....

Coconut, sprinkles,
Or butterscotch drops,
And pink-and-white frosting
To plop right on top.

What makes you goofy?
What makes you titter?
To trade silly faces
With Curly Bear's sitter!

A Twiddlebugs' picnic
With muffins and honey?

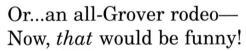

Or...an all-Grover rodeo—
Now, *that* would be funny!

What makes you giggle—
Makes you feel really good?
Just a regular day,
In your own neighborhood!

THE END

S is for School!

By P.J. Shaw • Illustrated by Joe Mathieu

Hello, Dorothy! Today was Elmo's first day of school. What's that, Dorothy? You want to know what it's like on the very first day of school? Elmo will tell you.

The first day of school is *so* exciting!

Just getting there is an adventure!

Some monsters wonder what to do
on the first day of school.

So it helps to have a buddy. Furry ones are fun!

At school, you might feel a little lonely now and then.

But a smile helps you make new friends.
A smile—and some crayons!

On the first day of school, a little fish can get homesick... so bring a picture for company. Guess what? Elmo brings a picture of Dorothy!

On the first day of school you see lots of new faces.

Lots of *friendly* faces! Yay!

The *end* of the first day of school is exciting, too.

It's a good time
for sharing what you've learned...

...with a friend!

⚬ THE END ⚬

Sleep Tight

By Constance Allen • Illustrated by David Prebenna

"Time to go home, Elmo!" calls Elmo's daddy.
"Just one more game of monster tag, please, Daddy?" asks Elmo.
"Okay. One more game," says Elmo's daddy.

On the way home from the park, Elmo and his daddy see lots of other people on their way home, too.
It's almost bedtime for little monsters.

On Sesame Street, everyone is getting ready for bed.

Splish, splash! Little Bird shakes his feathers in his warm bath.

Sleepy monsters comb their fur
and brush their teeth.

Flossie isn't sleepy yet. Herry and Flossie do stretches.

"... Seven, eight, nine, ten," pants Herry Monster. "Are you getting sleepy, Flossie?"

Flossie shakes her head.

"Ten slow toe touches," says Herry. "One... two... three... four..."

Oscar finishes his book, *Mother Grouch Rhymes*.
    "Little Boy Grouch, come blow your kazoo.
    Take a mud bath and eat anchovy stew…"
He closes his book.
Sleep tight, sleepy grouch.

Big Bird sings his teddy bear a lullaby.
"Rock-a-bye, Radar, snug in my nest.
Time for us both to lie down and rest!
Sleep tight, little bear," says Big Bird.

At the Snuffleupagus cave, it's bedtime
for Alice.
Boing! Boing! Boing!
She bounces on the bed.
Sleep tight, Alice.

In the Count's castle, the Count counts sheep.
"One sheep! Two sheep! Three beautiful woolly
sheep!" cries the Count.
Sleep tight, Count.

In the country, Cowboy Grover settles
down to sleep under the stars.
"Sleep tight, little cows!" he calls.

In the city, Hoots the Owl plays a saxophone serenade above the city lights.

Bee-boop-a-diddly-diddly-doo-wha-doo!

"I'll keep things cool till morning," he croons. "Sleep tight, everyone."

In Ernie's window box, sleepy Twiddlebugs
snuggle under their leaf blankets.
Sleep tight, little Twiddlebugs.

All is quiet on Sesame Street. Monsters and birds and grouches and Twiddlebugs sleep soundly in their beds.

Sleep tight, little Elmo.

THE END